CALICO ILLUSTRATED CLASSICS

Nathaniel Hawthorne's

# The **House** of the **Seven Gables**

ADAPTED BY: Jan Fields
ILLUSTRATED BY: Eric Scott Fisher

magic
wagon

## visit us at www.abdopublishing.com

Published by Magic Wagon, a division of the ABDO Group,
8000 West 78th Street, Edina, Minnesota 55439. Copyright
© 2011 by Abdo Consulting Group, Inc. International copyrights
reserved in all countries.

Calico Chapter Books™ is a trademark and logo of Magic Wagon.

Printed in the United States of America, Melrose Park, Illinois.
042010
092010

Original text by Nathaniel Hawthorne
Adapted by Jan Fields
Illustrated by Eric Scott Fisher
Edited by Stephanie Hedlund and Rochelle Baltzer
Cover and interior design by Abbey Fitzgerald

**Library of Congress Cataloging-in-Publication Data**

Fields, Jan.
  Nathaniel Hawthorne's The house of the seven gables / adapted by
Jan Fields ; illustrated by Eric Scott Fisher.
     p. cm. -- (Calico illustrated classics)
  Summary: A prominent New England family suffering under a two-
hundred-year-old curse is plagued by greed, vengeful acts, and violent
death.
  ISBN 978-1-60270-746-7
  [1. Secrets--Fiction. 2. Families--Fiction. 3. Haunted houses--Fiction.
4. New England--History--19th century--Fiction. 5. Horror stories.]
I. Fisher, Eric Scott, ill. II. Hawthorne, Nathaniel, 1804-1864. House
of the seven gables. III. Title. IV. Title: House of the seven gables.
  PZ7.F479177Nat 2010
  [Fic]--dc22
                                                    2010002614

# Table of Contents

# The Old Pyncheon Family

Halfway down a narrow New England street stands a rusty, wooden house with seven high-peaked gables. The gables face different directions like squabbling sisters with their backs against a single chimney. Directly in front of the house, a wide elm overshadows the main entrance. The street, the house, and even the elm are known by the name of Pyncheon.

With its faded glory, the house looks haunted by its past. Perhaps it is. This grand house was not the first home to sit on this spot. A shaggy thatched cottage once stood in its very spot. It was owned by Matthew Maule.

A stern Puritan leader named Colonel Pyncheon wanted the land. His desire grew despite Maule's stubborn refusal to sell. Eventually, Maule met the fate of many whose property became interesting to rich Puritan leaders—he was accused of witchcraft.

Some have said that Maule did have access to mysterious powers. At any rate, Maule was found guilty and was soon executed. Colonel Pyncheon went to the execution, and Maule spoke a last chilly prophecy as he pointed a shaking finger toward the colonel. "God will give him blood to drink!"

This prediction made many townspeople nervous, but not the stern colonel. He built the great house with its seven gables right on the spot of Maule's cottage. He even dared to hire Maule's own son to oversee work on the house. Then Pyncheon threw a party.

On the day of the party, food and drink flowed freely to the guests. They had only one cause for complaint—the old man never showed himself at his own party!

Finally, the lieutenant governor arrived and expected to be greeted by his host. He demanded explanation for Pyncheon's absence. A servant explained that the colonel had ordered that he not be disturbed.

"Colonel Pyncheon has simply lost track of the time," the aristocrat insisted. "He will want to be told of my arrival."

"Even so," the servant said nervously, "my master's orders were clear and I dare not vary from them."

"Pooh," said the lieutenant governor. "I will take the matter into my own hands." And the man stomped loudly to the colonel's door with a cluster of guests following him. He pounded on the door several times with no response.

"Very strange," the man muttered. As he turned the door handle, a gust of wind flung the door open wide.

Colonel Pyncheon sat in an oaken chair beneath a huge portrait of himself. At first, the portrait and the man seemed to glare together

at the group. But then, the colonel's young grandson darted into the room. He made his way halfway to the glaring figure when he stopped and began screaming.

Pyncheon's beard was soaked through with blood, and more blood ran down his collar. The iron-hearted old Puritan was dead! A single sentence passed among the group in whispered awe, "God hath given him blood to drink!"

Now, the heirs of Colonel Pyncheon received his house and wealth, but one thing they did not get as they expected. The colonel had spoken often of his ownership of a great piece of land in Maine. This land would be of enormous worth, but the paperwork to support it was never found.

Over the years, it became less and less likely such papers would be honored even if they were found. But the story of this great land was handed down from Pyncheon to Pyncheon to be dreamed about and longed for.

The Pyncheon wealth seemed to grow less with each generation, while misfortune increased. One elderly Pyncheon had the misfortune of being murdered by his own nephew—or so the courts decided before sending the young man to prison.

Finally, there remained only one truly wealthy Pyncheon heir. This heir was a lawyer with the same grasping nature of the original ancestor.

Such a grand family was reduced to a lawyer, a murderer, a young country cousin, and the sole inhabitant of the Pyncheon house: an elderly spinster. And it is with her that we begin.

# The Little Shop Window

Before sunrise, Miss Hepzibah Pyncheon stood in front of her mirror and glared at her image. She was a pale, thin, rusty-jointed maiden of sixty years. But, she was no more unhappy with her appearance than she had been at any hour of her life.

Her scowl was habit, not anger. Miss Hepzibah's vision was poor and the constant scowl came from her efforts to see beyond the end of her own nose.

Though she looked hard and bitter, nothing could be further from the truth. She was tender-hearted and devoted to her brother, though he was far away and in horrible circumstance. Her only character flaws were shyness and more than a little family pride.

Hepzibah glanced at a miniature of her gentle, beautiful brother. "Don't be ashamed of me," she whispered. "I'm doing this for you."

She hurried through the darkened passages of the house, pausing only once in a shadowy parlor. The room contained some antique tables and uncomfortable chairs scattered about on the worn carpet. There were only three truly noteworthy pieces: a framed map of the mythic Pyncheon holdings in Maine, a fine oak chair, and the portrait of old Colonel Pyncheon.

Miss Hepzibah glared up at the portrait and then bowed her head. What would Colonel Pyncheon think of what she was about to do? She shook herself and hurried on to her destination.

On the lowest level, in a gable facing the street, a Pyncheon had set up a shop nearly a century before. The shop was closed soon after and left undisturbed for many years as the family tried to forget such a blot on their history. The Pyncheons were not shopkeepers!

And yet, Miss Hepzibah had polished the floors and counters of the shop. She had stocked it with trinkets and toys. Gingerbread elephants tramped across the windowsill. Tall barrels of flour, apples, and cornmeal stood in a neat row near the counter. The antique scale was as polished as rust and ruin would allow.

Like many aging gentlewomen, Miss Hepzibah was opening a shop. She already had a small income from renting part of the house to a young photographer. But that brought in so little she was forced to seek other income or starve. Yet no occupation seemed less suited to the shy, scowling woman than selling things.

Miss Hepzibah had considered her options. Her hands trembled too much to be a seamstress. She had toyed with the idea of opening a school, but she simply did not like children. They frightened her, and she suspected that modern children actually knew more than she.

As Miss Hepzibah bustled around the shop, her sighs came so rapidly that it seemed she must be a thing of steam and not a human at all. Finally, she hauled the bar free from the door and hung an open sign with trembling hands.

This last action seemed to sap the last of Hepzibah's courage. She dashed back into the house, threw herself in the oak chair, and wept.

As Miss Hepzibah Pyncheon sat on the oak chair with her hands over her face, she heard a terrifying sound. The little bell suspended over the shop door tinkled. Her first customer had arrived!

She leaped to her feet and rushed into the shop. With her pale face and scowl, she looked better prepared to face a burglar than a customer.

The customer stood in the doorway. It was a slender young man in his early twenties with a brown beard and mustache. He wore a simple summer suit and a straw hat. He met the scowl of Miss Hepzibah without alarm, as he had seen it many times before. This was the boarder in her house.

"My dear Miss Pyncheon," he said, "I am glad to see you have begun your adventure. Best wishes. How may I help you on this first day?"

The old woman took one look at the kind face and burst into tears. "Oh, Mr. Holgrave, I wish I were dead," she wailed.

"Oh, believe me, Miss Hepzibah, these feelings will pass," he said. "I believe this is the best thing you could do. It will pull you out of the shadows and warm your veins. Trust me."

"I do not understand such modern notions," she said. "And I do not wish to."

"Then we shall never more speak of them," he said kindly. "But I believe you are doing a brave thing. And I have come to purchase biscuits for breakfast."

"Let me be a lady a moment longer," Hepzibah said with a rare smile. "A Pyncheon

must not take money from her only friend for a morsel of bread."

With his wrapped parcel, Holgrave slipped out, leaving a much cheerier Hepzibah. But it was a short-lived cheer, as she overheard two workmen chattering outside her door.

"See here, Dixey!" cried one rough voice. "Trade seems to be looking up on Pyncheon Street!"

The second man made a rude noise. "That old woman's face is enough to frighten Old Nick himself. I can't imagine customers standing for such a glare."

"These cent shops never come to much," the first man said glumly. "My wife kept one for three months and lost five dollars!"

"Poor business," replied Dixey as they walked on. "Poor business."

Hepzibah found herself hurt by their prediction of doom for her business. She was more hurt still that they seemed so casual about her ruin.

The shop bell tinkled again. A sturdy little boy marched in with his school slate under his arm. He stopped short as Hepzibah scowled down at him.

"Well, child," she said, "what did you want?"

"The gingerbread man in the window," he said, holding out his cent.

Hepzibah handed the child the cookie and waved away his penny. She could not imagine taking a small child's pocket money for a bit of stale gingerbread.

The boy dashed outside, leaving the door wide open as he bit the head off his cookie. Hepzibah grumbled as she marched over to close the door and replace the gingerbread man with another.

No sooner had she gotten the door closed than the bell rang again. The boy was back. Crumbs decorated his face and clothes. "I want that one too," he said, pointing at the new cookie.

Miss Hepzibah suspected this could go on all day, so she asked for his penny. He turned it over and carried the second sweet out of the shop. Miss Hepzibah stared at the penny in her hand. She had done it. She was the keeper of a cent shop.

# CHAPTER 3

# A Day Behind the Counter

As more customers came and went, many had complaints. Hepzibah's cotton thread was rotten. She had no tobacco. Five people left in a huff after learning she had no root beer.

Toward noon, Hepzibah caught sight of a tall, portly gentleman across the street. He stared toward the House of the Seven Gables as he mopped his bald head with a bit of linen.

When he caught Hepzibah's eye, his frown turned to a smile of the sunniest good humor. He bowed to her and she answered his smile with a deeper scowl.

"Go away, Cousin Jaffrey," she whispered. "I will do as I like. Pyncheon House is my own while I'm alive!"

The gentleman walked toward the shop. He clearly intended to visit, but his path was blocked when the young gingerbread lover dashed ahead of him to buy a gingerbread elephant for his lunch. The man passed on down the street instead.

Hepzibah looked after him, murmuring, "The smile does not fool me. Let Jaffrey Pyncheon beware lest he draw down the Pyncheon curse again."

Again, the shop bell rang. This time it signaled the arrival of a thin, ancient figure known in the neighborhood as Uncle Venner. He had seemed old even when Hepzibah was a girl. The simple old man thought himself wise and often gave advice during his visits.

"So, you have really begun trade," he said. "Well, I'm glad to see it. Young people should never live idle in the world."

"Thank you, Uncle Venner," Hepzibah said, smiling. She had not been called young for some time.

"I met your cousin, the judge," the old man said. "He bowed to me. He has a most remarkable smile."

"Yes," Hepzibah said tightly. "My cousin is thought to be pleasant."

Uncle Venner nodded and said, "I must say, I'm surprised one such as the judge would let a cousin fall upon hard times."

"My store has nothing to do with my cousin," she said.

"Well," the old man said, "I expect it will be short enough. Something better will turn up for you, I'm sure of it!" Suddenly the old man gestured her close. "When do you expect him home?"

"Whom do you mean?" she asked faintly.

"Ah, I see you don't want to talk of it," he said. "No matter, though there is talk of it all over town. I remember him, Miss Hepzibah."

The old man left Hepzibah in a cloud of confusion. She seemed to pass the rest of the day as in a dream, making mistakes with nearly every customer. It was a great relief when the time came to close the shop for the night after making one last sale of gingerbread to her most faithful young customer.

As she closed up, she spotted a carriage pulling up before the house. For an instant, Hepzibah held her breath, thinking it might be him home now. But a lively young woman in a

cheerful straw bonnet sprang from it. The driver carried her bags to the door of the house.

"This must be Phoebe," Hepzibah muttered, for she often talked to herself in the empty house. "She has the look of her father about her. How like country cousins to visit without a warning. Well, she can only stay one night," Hepzibah insisted as she unbolted the door. "If Clifford were to find her here, it might disturb him."

# May and November

Phoebe Pyncheon awoke when the crimson glow of sunrise crept between the curtains of her bed. At first, she did not recognize the room or the heavy bed curtains.

As she climbed from the bed, memories of her arrival and chat with Hepzibah came to mind. Phoebe had told Hepzibah that her mother's second marriage made it better if Phoebe moved to another home.

Phoebe dressed quickly and peeped out the window to see that her room overlooked the garden. She saw a tall rosebush covered with beautiful white roses. Hurrying down the creaking staircase, she found her way to the garden. She gathered a great armload of the most perfect of the roses and brought them to brighten her room.

Then, Phoebe went in search of Hepzibah. When Phoebe found her, her elder cousin drew a deep breath and said, "Cousin Phoebe, I really can't see my way clear to keep you with me."

"Dear cousin," Phoebe said, "we may suit one another much better than you suppose."

"This is no environment for a young person," Hepzibah said. "The dust and decay of this old house is unwholesome for the lungs."

"Then I shall busy myself in the garden every day," Phoebe observed. "That should keep me healthy."

"Perhaps," the old woman said. "But it is not my decision to make. The master of this house is soon coming."

"Judge Pyncheon?" Phoebe asked, confused.

"No, no!" Hepzibah shouted. "He is not welcome to cross this threshold while I live. I speak of Clifford Pyncheon. Look, I will show you." She retrieved a miniature portrait and handed it to Phoebe.

"He is very beautiful," Phoebe said. "He has as sweet a face as a man can have. But I thought I had heard . . . I thought Clifford Pyncheon had died long ago."

"Perhaps he has," Hepzibah said. "In old houses like this, the dead are apt to come back." She sighed and patted her young cousin's hand. "You are welcome to such a home as I can offer at present." And at this, the old woman kissed her cheek.

The two women went downstairs, where Phoebe bustled about the kitchen preparing a most lovely breakfast. Before they left the breakfast table, the shop bell rang sharply and Hepzibah moaned. Though the day before had been difficult, the thought of returning to the shop was almost unbearable.

"Do not trouble yourself, dear cousin," cried Phoebe. "I will be shopkeeper today."

Phoebe proved to be good as her word, bustling about the shop with the same cheerful energy she had shown over breakfast. She charmed every customer until even the crankiest left with a smile.

During a lull in business, Phoebe showed Hepzibah a list of ideas for improving the business.

"I can make yeast, both liquid and in cakes," Phoebe said. "I can make spice cakes to sell and brew the beer our customers ask after. We must renew our stock of gingerbread figures. And we've had at least a dozen requests for molasses candy."

"Well done. Well done," said Uncle Venner, who had shuffled in and out of the shop several times during the morning. "Bless my eyes, what a brisk little soul!"

"Yes, she is a nice girl," Hepzibah said. "But not at all like a Pyncheon."

"Not like any I've met," the old man agreed.

As the day passed, the two cousins grew quite fond of each other. After the shop was closed for the day, Hepzibah took Phoebe on a tour of the house. As they walked, the old woman told Phoebe of the boarder.

"He has the strangest companions who dress in newfangled and ill-fitting garments," Hepzibah said. "And he speaks of the oddest things."

She went on to explain that she suspected the man practiced animal magnetism, hypnosis, and other dark arts.

"Then why would you let him stay?" Phoebe asked.

"He is a quiet sort of person," Hepzibah said. "And he has such a way of taking hold of one's mind. I would be sorry to lose sight of him entirely."

Phoebe argued no more against the young man, but still she wondered.

# Chapter 5

# Maule's Well

After an early tea, Phoebe returned to the garden. Though it was overgrown, she saw that someone had set to taming its wildness. The white rosebush had clearly been propped up recently. A pear and three plum trees had been pruned. And though the flower beds were a mess, they showed signs of recent weeding.

As she wandered around the garden, Phoebe saw more signs of attention. A vegetable patch flourished with squash vines filled with orange blossoms. Phoebe wondered whose hand had been the gardener. She could little imagine Hepzibah kneeling and pulling weeds.

She walked deeper into the garden and found an overgrown fountain with a rim of old mossy stones. Its bed was paved with colored pebbles. She turned from the fountain and spotted a henhouse.

The henhouse was the home of Chanticleer, his two wives, and a solitary chicken. These represented the last of the purebred chicken of the Pyncheon family. Once this line had produced chickens as big as turkeys, but now they were little larger than pigeons. The hens had a rusty, withered look.

Phoebe ran into the house to collect crumbs and scraps for the chickens. "Here, you odd little chickens," she called to them gently. "Here are some nice crumbs for you." A chicken gathered enough life to flutter up and alight on Phoebe's shoulder.

"You are much favored!" said a voice behind Phoebe.

Turning quickly, Phoebe was surprised to see a young man with a hoe. She knew this must be the photographer, Holgrave, who rented one

of the gables. He smiled as he used his hoe to draw up earth around the roots of the tomatoes.

"None of the chickens have shown me nearly so much friendliness," he said, "though I have fed them every day."

Phoebe smiled. "I have simply learned how to talk with hens and chickens."

"I think they recognize the family tone," the young man said. "You are a Pyncheon?"

"My name is Phoebe Pyncheon," she said. "I see you have given much care to my cousin's garden."

"I would gladly share the chore with you," he said. "I have little interest in the flowers or chickens. I prefer to tend vegetables to add to the dinner pot."

To show her agreement with his idea, Phoebe began to pull weeds. She started in a flower bed close to the vegetable plantings.

"Has Miss Hepzibah told you I make pictures with light? Would you like to see a sample?" Holgrave asked.

"A daguerreotype likeness, you mean?" Phoebe asked. "I don't much like pictures of that sort. They always seem so stern and hard."

The young man showed her a daguerreotype miniature in a morocco case. "I know that face," she said. "Its stern eye followed me from the parlor portrait all day. How did you make a picture of my Puritan ancestor without his skull cap and gray beard?"

Holgrave laughed. "This is a Pyncheon, though this man is still quite alive. He wears a smile always for the world's eye, but I think the camera has captured what lies in his heart."

"Then many dreadful things must lie there," Phoebe said with a shudder. "I don't wish to see it anymore. Not every Pyncheon looks so harsh. I have seen another miniature that shows someone I could not imagine ever looking so stern."

"Ah, you have seen Clifford's portrait. Hepzibah has told me about it, but she has not shown it to me," Holgrave said. "Is there nothing dark or sinister in the picture? Nothing dangerous or mad?"

Phoebe found Holgrave's mysterious tone unsettling and turned away.

"Wait," he called, though he moved toward the door to his own gable. "On any bright day, if you will put one of those rosebuds in your hair and come to my rooms in Central Street, I will make a picture of the flower and its wearer."

Phoebe looked after him thoughtfully.

"Be careful not to drink at Maule's well," he said, turning once more toward her.

"Is that it with the rim of mossy stones?" she asked. "Why not?"

"Its water is bewitched."

As the strange young man disappeared into the house, Phoebe went in as well. She found Hepzibah sitting in the darkness and went to the kitchen to fetch a lamp. She heard whispering above her.

"In a moment, cousin," she called.

But instead of a response from Hepzibah, she heard only more murmurings. She carried the lamp to the room where her cousin sat.

"My dear cousin," she said, "is there someone here with us?"

"Phoebe, my dear girl," Hepzibah said. "You've had a full day. You should get to bed." The old lady kissed the young girl, dismissing her.

As the young cousin turned in her bed, she heard heavy footsteps on the stairs and more murmurs.

# The Guest

Phoebe awoke to the twittering of the robins in the pear tree and the sound of movement below. She hurried down to find Hepzibah standing beside the kitchen window with a cookbook held close to her nose.

The old woman sighed and put the book down. "Do you know if Old Speckle has laid an egg?" she asked. "And do you suppose you could make coffee?"

Phoebe dashed out to the henhouse, but the hens had nothing to offer. When she returned, she saw Hepzibah rapping on the window and gesturing toward the fish dealer who stood on the street.

"I would like some mackerel," Hepzibah said.

"Here is the finest piece on my cart," the man said enthusiastically. "And as fat a one as ever I've had so early in the season."

"Good, good." The old woman rushed about the kitchen preparing the woodstove to receive the fish. In truth, Hepzibah had a complete horror of the stove, but this breakfast was so important she made a rush at it with the courage of a knight smiting a dragon.

"I could make a nice Indian cake," Phoebe offered. She had no idea why this breakfast above all others was so important to her elderly cousin.

"Good, good," Hepzibah said.

While the lovely smell of breakfast filled the air, several half-starved rats slipped out of their hiding places. They sat on their hind legs, sniffing the air and waiting for any opportunity to nibble.

The women carried the food and coffee to a small, ancient table draped with a cloth. "It must be perfect," the old woman fretted. "He so loves beautiful things." She looked at her young cousin. "And do smile. He'll enjoy your smile. Are there any flowers in the garden?"

Phoebe hurried out and gathered roses and a few other flowers. She arranged them in a glass pitcher to add a sweet air to the stuffy room. From the portrait over the table, the Puritan scowled down at them as if nothing on the table pleased him in the least.

Then, the women heard footsteps on the stairs. Hepzibah burst into tears from nerves.

"My dearest cousin, who is it?" Phoebe asked.

"Hush, hush, he is coming," the old woman whispered as she wiped the tears from her eyes. "My dear, dear Clifford."

At the words, the shuffling steps they heard finally produced a figure in the passageway. Phoebe saw an elderly man in an old-fashioned dressing gown. His gray hair hung to an unusual length and he looked around the room in confusion.

Hepzibah rushed to grasp his hands and lead him to the table, where he ate as if starved. "More, more," he cried. "This is what I need!"

Finally he slowed the pace of his eating and looked around more. Though Hepzibah gazed at him with devotion, his eyes always slipped quickly past her to rest on Phoebe.

"How pleasant! How delightful!" he murmured. Then his face darkened and he seemed to sink back into his confusion.

Phoebe snatched up one of the roses and held it out to him. "Here is a new kind of rose I found in the garden," she said. "It has a lovely scent."

"Ah, let me see!" He held the rose to his face, lost in pleasant memories. "Thank you, this has done me good." His eyes cleared a bit and he looked up at the scowling portrait. "Hepzibah, why must we look at that horrible picture? Take it down!"

"You know I cannot," she cried. "It is fast to the wall, but Phoebe will help me cover it in some lovely red velvet. You'll like that."

He smiled, but then shrieked when the shop bell rang. Phoebe hastened away to tend to the customer.

"How can you stand that clanging?" Clifford demanded.

Hepzibah told him gently that she kept a shop. "Is it such a shameful thing?" she asked.

"Shame! Talk not to me of shame!" he demanded. Then he burst into tears. Finally he slumped back in his well-padded chair and whispered, "Are we so very poor, Hepzibah?"

Hepzibah could not reply, but none was needed as Clifford drifted into sleep. With tears running down her cheeks, she let down the curtain over the sunny window. Then she slipped from the room, leaving Clifford to his dreams.

# The Pyncheon of Today

Phoebe entered the shop to find her faithful gingerbread customer on an errand for his mother. He had spent his entire life savings on gingerbread in the past two days. Phoebe filled his mother's order and added a gingerbread whale as a gift.

The boy grinned and dashed out of the shop, passing a portly gentleman in rich clothes. The man strutted in with a smile.

"Oh," he said, clearly surprised to see Phoebe. "You must be Hepzibah's assistant. I did not know her shop fared so well."

"I am her assistant," Phoebe said, "and her cousin."

"Cousin? Oh, yes, I can see dear Arthur's look about you," the big man said. "Then I am also your cousin, Judge Pyncheon!" With that, the judge leaned forward as if to kiss Phoebe. The girl stepped back, leaving the judge kissing the air like a fish.

At this, his sunny smile darkened. Then, Phoebe recognized him as the face in the picture from the garden.

"I approve," the judge said, smiling again. "A young girl must guard her kisses. Do tell me, cousin, has Hepzibah's brother arrived? I heard he had." He paused and his smile grew even wider. "I see by your face that he has. I shall pop in to see him."

"Perhaps I should get Hepzibah first," Phoebe said. "The dear man is napping now. I am sure Hepzibah would not like him disturbed."

Again the judge's face darkened. "You tell me how to behave around my two dear cousins whom I have known since we were all children?" he demanded. "You are more a stranger to them than I, my dear. I am family, and I will go see my cousin."

The deep boom of his voice had carried to the parlor, where Hepzibah watched over her brother. She rushed out with a scowl so fierce that the judge actually stepped back from her.

"Hepzibah, I am rejoiced at Clifford's return," the big man said, recovering quickly. "I have come to offer the comfort of my home for Clifford's recovery."

Phoebe was so delighted with the judge's kind offer that she felt rather bad about not letting him kiss her. Hepzibah reacted quite differently, nearly choking as she said, "Clifford has a home here!"

"We shall ask him," the judge said, advancing on Hepzibah. "Make way! I must see Clifford."

Hepzibah spread out her gaunt figure across the door and seemed to increase in bulk. She trembled at the cost of standing up to such a man as Judge Pyncheon, for she truly was a

gentle and shy woman. Still, she could not allow him access to her brother.

At this moment, a helpless wail rose from the parlor beyond. "Hepzibah," cried the trembling voice, "don't let him in. I could not bear it. Oh, let him have mercy on me. Mercy!"

At the sound of a voice so feeble, so helpless, a red fire kindled in the judge's eyes. He stepped forward like a predator that had finally cornered his prey after a fierce hunt.

Phoebe gasped at the change in the man. The judge swung sharply back again to the smiling picture of kindness.

"Cousin Hepzibah," he said, "you do me a very great wrong. But I forgive it. Clearly he is too tired from his journey. I will return later."

With a bow to Hepzibah and a parting nod to Phoebe, the judge left the shop. As soon as he passed out of sight, Hepzibah began to shake.

"Oh, Phoebe," she murmured as she embraced her young cousin. "That man has been the horror of my life."

"His offer seemed kind," Phoebe said.

"Do not speak of his offers," Hepzibah spat. She patted the young girl gently. "Do go amuse Clifford and quiet him while I compose myself. It would frighten him to see me like this."

Phoebe went, but she thought often in the days ahead about what she had seen.

# Clifford and Phoebe

After the judge's attempted visit, Hepzibah took every opportunity to bring beautiful things to Clifford. He had loved books as a young man, so Hepzibah unlocked a bookcase and took down several books. She thought she'd read aloud to Clifford.

Sadly, the old woman's voice had grown so rough with age that it sounded more like the croak of a crow than the song of a lark. She added a rough, dismal air to every word she read. Clifford soon waved her off.

Desperate, she considered thrumming on the chords of the old harpsichord. She had little memory of the lessons she had taken as a child, but she was willing to try. Perhaps a whispered word from the ghost of Alice Pyncheon, who had owned the harpsichord, turned her away from the idea. At any rate, she did not subject Clifford's nerves to the sound.

The worst thing of all for Hepzibah was Clifford's refusal to look at her. She had never been lovely and time had done her no favors. She considered putting bright ribbons on the dull clothes she wore, but again something caused her to turn away from the idea.

In the end, she settled upon having Phoebe be Clifford's nursemaid and playmate. He doted upon her, and his mood lightened every time the young girl entered the room.

Phoebe had a great love for singing and a lovely voice. Clifford so enjoyed the sound. He kept his light mood as long as she would sing as she went about her chores.

Thus Phoebe swept away much of the air of decay and shadow in the old house. She threw open curtains and pried open windows to the healthful air.

In all this, Hepzibah never showed a drop of jealousy. Instead, she was deeply grateful that Phoebe could bring her brother pleasure. Hepzibah's devotion to her brother was complete.

Phoebe sometimes drooped in the heavy atmosphere about her, but her naturally sunny nature soon overcame. She responded to Clifford out of her kind heart, stirred simply by his need for it.

And so the family settled into a routine—Hepzibah watched over her brother during his long, frequent naps. Then, Phoebe lightened his mood whenever he woke.

Were it up to Clifford, he would have spent every day seated in his plush chair in the parlor. But Phoebe seldom failed in coaxing him out to the garden. Mr. Holgrave and Uncle Venner had repaired the summerhouse until it was quite a pleasant spot.

Phoebe often read to Clifford from fiction pamphlets and poetry books lent to her by

Holgrave. Clifford enjoyed the sound of her voice but little followed the stories. When Phoebe laughed at words on the page, Clifford looked confused. And if a story brought her to tears, he demanded she put the book away.

Clifford never failed to ask what flowers had bloomed in the new day. His feeling for flowers was intense and he often sat with one in his hand, studying it.

He also loved the happy buzz of bees as they set about collecting nectar. He delighted in the hummingbirds, which hovered over a thick climbing bean vine covered with vivid scarlet flowers.

But more than all this, Clifford loved the chickens. He insisted they be set free to wander the garden. He couldn't stand to see them confined. The chickens seemed to converse constantly in clucks and grumbles as they set about clearing Maule's well of snails.

During the week, Phoebe and Clifford were often the only occupants of the summerhouse, though Hepzibah would slip in now and then. But on Sundays, after Phoebe had been to church, they had a kind of festival in the garden.

Holgrave would join them along with Uncle Venner. Clifford seemed to enjoy the ancient neighbor especially. Perhaps the old man made Clifford feel younger in comparison.

At some point in each gathering, Hepzibah and Phoebe would bring out a china bowl of currants, freshly gathered and crushed with sugar. These were all the refreshments available, but they were well received.

"Miss Hepzibah, ma'am," Uncle Venner said one day, "I really enjoy these quiet meetings of a Sabbath afternoon."

"And we benefit from your visits," Hepzibah assured him.

Holgrave also took great pains to talk with Clifford in a cheerful way. Still, the artist's deep, thoughtful eyes seemed to pry into the old man as if looking for something inside.

Certainly though, when the young artist set his mind on lightening the mood, the entire party found themselves cheerier. Phoebe often thought, *How pleasant he can be!* Even Hepzibah would smile with something almost youthful about her face.

During these garden parties, Clifford was the most cheerful of all in the bright sunshine. But when the shadows of late afternoon began to touch the garden, so did the excitement fade from Clifford's eyes.

"I want my happiness," he often murmured. "Many, many years have I waited for it! It is late! I want my happiness!"

# CHAPTER
## 9

# The Arched Window

Though Clifford made no request for variety in his days, Phoebe felt it might benefit him to experience different things. She urged him up the stairs to look out upon the street from the great arched window on the second floor.

This window had once opened onto a balcony, but the railing had long ago decayed. Still, Clifford would sit with the window flung wide open and watch the comings and goings of the street. He kept himself partially hidden by the long draperies.

Clifford seemed to view each event on the street as completely new. Every time the bus passed, he reacted with amazement. And though the water cart passed two or three times a day to wet the dusty streets, Clifford viewed each pass as a novelty.

Only the handcarts brought real memory to the front. Clifford smiled down at the butcher's cart with its snowy canopy. The harsh bells of the baker's cart brought a cheery glance. And the old man reacted to the horrid screech of the scissor grinder as if it were music. These things stripped away the years and brought Clifford moments of childhood again.

His reactions to things were often mixed. The Italian boy with his barrel organ always got his full attention. But the organ grinder's monkey with its dark, pinched face and long, thick tail produced a different effect. Clifford seemed fearful of it or disgusted as it begged for coins.

Then one day, a political parade clogged the streets. It filled the air with the sounds of drums, fifes, and cymbals. From the window, it seemed a mighty river of people passed below, calling them with the clang and rattle.

Clifford shuddered and grew pale. He threw an appealing look at Hepzibah and Phoebe. They thought he was alarmed at the strangeness.

At last, he stood up and set his foot on the windowsill. In an instant more, he would have been in the unguarded balcony. Had he made it to the balcony, he would probably have leaped into the street. The women grabbed his garments and held him back.

Hepzibah shrieked, "Clifford, are you crazy?"

"I hardly know, Hepzibah," the old man said as he allowed them to lead him back to his chair. "It is over now, but I do believe that if I had taken that plunge, it would have made me another man."

One of Clifford's favorite times to watch the street was early Sunday mornings. The church bells called over the whole city, scattering the blessed sounds.

Clifford sat at the window with Hepzibah, watching the neighbors as they stepped into the street. Phoebe joined the parade of those

hurrying to church. She threw an upward glance and smiled with her familiar gladness.

"Hepzibah, do you never go to church?" asked Clifford, after watching Phoebe walk to the corner.

"No, Clifford," she replied. "Not these many, many years."

"Were I to be there," he said, "I could pray once more in the company of so many human souls."

"Dear brother," she replied, "let us go!"

So Hepzibah and her brother made themselves ready in their old-fashioned finery. They went down the stairs together and pulled open the front door. Then, they stepped across the threshold into the presence of the whole world. There they froze.

"It cannot be," the old man said, with deep sadness. "We are ghosts. We have no right among the living."

They shrank back into the dark house.

Don't think that Clifford was always sad. He enjoyed watching children through the window. One day, he called to Hepzibah and Phoebe that he would like to blow bubbles.

The bright bubbles floated down from the window, and landed softly on passersby. Some greeted them with joy. Others with irritation.

One especially large bubble floated down to settle upon the nose of an elderly gentleman in fine clothes. The man scowled up to find the source of the bubble, and then smiled.

"Aha, Cousin Clifford!" he said. "Still blowing soap bubbles?"

The tone seemed almost kind. But behind it was something bitter and cruel. Clifford shrank back in terror without quite knowing why.

# CHAPTER
## 10

# The Daguerreotypist

Like many elderly invalids, Clifford usually retired to rest while the sunbeams were still melting through his window curtains. This meant Phoebe had late afternoons and early evenings free to follow her own tastes.

Like many young New England women, she attended lectures, listened to concerts, and went shopping. She sometimes ransacked entire depots of splendid merchandise and brought home a ribbon.

Though these outings helped keep the cheerful good humor that she had brought to the house, Phoebe was changing. She was growing from a girl to a woman. Her eyes looked larger and darker and deeper, like wells.

She often spent time with the daguerreotypist. She was not certain that she knew him well, though they talked nearly every day. He shared stories of his life, but something still seemed hidden about him. Phoebe never doubted his integrity, only suspected he held to a moral code that might not be her own.

Holgrave told her he could not boast of his origins as they were very humble. Left early on his own, he had become a self-dependent boy.

Though now just short of twenty-two years, he had been first a country schoolmaster, then a shopkeeper, then the political editor of a country newspaper. He had traveled throughout New England as a peddler of cologne water. He had briefly studied and practiced dentistry with great success in the factory towns along the inland streams.

He had traveled to Europe while working on a packet ship. He had been a lecturer on the science of hypnosis. "I was known to be quite gifted at mesmerism," he assured her.

Now his job of daguerreotypist was likely to last no longer than his previous occupations. He was foremost an adventurer who looked always for change.

"It is odd for one who so loves change to seek lodging at so old and unchanged a house," Phoebe said.

"Had I the choice," he said. "I would burn it to the ground. I think it unwise that humans live so much with the cold ruling hand of dead men."

"Dead men?" Phoebe echoed.

"We follow laws set by dead men. We live in homes built by dead men. We adorn ourselves with ornaments collected by dead men. We even worship the living god according to the rules and rituals set forth by dead men."

The young man's face grew red as he spoke passionately. A passerby looking into the garden might imagine the young man was declaring his love for Phoebe instead of ranting about the dead.

"I do not see it that way," Phoebe said gently.

"I believe houses should be made to last no more than twenty years," the young man said. "That we might be reminded not only to rebuild the structure but to rebuild the institutions they symbolize."

Phoebe shook her head in dismay. "It would make me dizzy to think of such a shifting world. And it makes me wonder again why you lodge in this house and with these people. You

ask daily after Clifford's health and happiness. Why your interest in a family that seems to represent the very things you dislike?"

"I study them," Holgrave said. "This is an odd and incomprehensible world and as I look at it, I learn about it. People are a riddle that I seek always to solve. People say the Pyncheons are cursed and I wish to understand that, too."

Phoebe's brow darkened. She disliked hearing her kinsmen spoken of like creatures to be examined and weighed.

"Do you not worry about catching the family lunacy?" she asked.

Holgrave laughed. "Perhaps I have already caught it. It may be that I am a bit mad. Do you know the history of the Pyncheons?"

"I have heard it from my mother," she said. "And Hepzibah has told me many times since my arrival here."

"I have an incident of Pyncheon family history that I have written in the form of a legend," he said. "I mean to have it published in a magazine."

"You write for magazines?" she asked.

"You did not know? So much for my literary fame," he said, laughing again. "Would you like to hear it?"

"Yes, if it is not so terribly long," Phoebe said with a laugh of her own. "Nor very dull."

And so the young man brought out his manuscript and began to read.

# Holgrave's Tale

One day, a message arrived for Matthew Maule, the carpenter. His presence was desired at the House of the Seven Gables.

"And what does your master want from me?" he asked Mr. Pyncheon's servant.

"The master does not tell me his wishes," the servant, Scipio, answered. "But it must be a very good house or the old master would not haunt it and scare poor servants so."

"The house is haunted?" the carpenter asked. "Go tell your master I am coming."

Scipio turned, but Maule called him back. "If you happen to see Mistress Alice, his daughter, give her Matthew Maule's humble respects."

The servant left in a huff. He felt a lowly workman had no right to even mention Alice Pyncheon.

The young carpenter was the grandson of the former Matthew Maule. Some muttered that young Maule had inherited his grandfather's magic. He could see into the dreams of others, some whispered. He could stare into your mind and see your thoughts, others claimed. He had the evil eye that brought blight to corn and death to children.

After receiving Mr. Pyncheon's message, the carpenter finished the project he had begun. Then he made his way to the House of the Seven Gables. As he approached, he saw the house was well cared for and bustling with life. He spied little work for a carpenter.

At an open window on the second floor, Alice Pyncheon leaned out to tend some pots of exotic flowers. She looked just as exotic and lovely as they did.

Maule looked up at the sundial that hung above the front gable. Its creeping shadow showed the passing time. He decided it showed that it was time he learned what the Pyncheons could want with him.

Now, the proper entry point for young Maule would have been a rear entrance. But Maule stormed up to the front door and pounded the iron knocker.

Scipio opened the door in a rush to see who pounded.

"Here I am," Maule said. "Show me to your master."

The servant scowled but led the carpenter quickly to the parlor. Mr. Pyncheon had filled the room with stylish furniture from Europe. Yet, the scowling face of his Puritan grandfather glared down at him in obvious disapproval.

"You wanted me?" Maule demanded.

Mr. Pyncheon looked calmly at the young carpenter. "You know of the claim my grandfather held on lands to the east?"

"I had heard of them," Maule said.

"There is a story," Pyncheon said, "that your father knew the whereabouts of the papers that proved this claim. And if this is the case, perhaps you might know as well. I would pay well for these papers."

Maule smiled. "I could find the papers and give them to you, in exchange for this house and the land it is on."

At first, Mr. Pyncheon was inclined to take offense at Maule's demand. But in truth, Pyncheon hated New England and especially the old house. It reminded him of the horror of discovering his bloody grandfather when he was a child. He had only returned to the house because he could no longer afford to live abroad.

"I consent to your proposition," he said finally.

"Then call down your daughter," the carpenter said. "I can only find the papers if I have the use of a clear and perfect mind."

This hit Pyncheon as a much harder demand, but he did want the papers very badly. The wealth from the eastern lands would benefit Alice as much as himself, so he sent for her.

Alice was summoned and appeared. As she came into the room, her eyes fell upon the carpenter. A glow of artistic approval brightened her face as she admired the strength and energy of Maule's figure.

Many men would have been delighted to catch such an admiring glance from Alice Pyncheon, but Maule was not like many men.

*The girl looks at me as if I were a beast for sale,* he thought. *She shall know what form of man I am when my spirit proves stronger than hers.*

"You sent for me, Father?" she asked.

"Your business is with me," Maule said, drawing her attention sharply.

She turned toward her father in surprise.

"Yes, Alice," the older man said, frowning. "This young man is Matthew Maule. He said he can find an important document, but he needs you to do so. I ask that you oblige me and answer his inquiries."

"As you will remain in the room," Maule said, "I am certain Mistress Alice will feel herself quite safe."

"I certainly feel no anxiety with my father at hand," she said calmly. "And I am not afraid of you at any rate."

"Then, please sit down and fix your eyes on mine."

Her father turned away nervously. Was it safe to trust Alice in this person's hands? And yet, they needed those papers very much. As he pondered this, he heard a small cry from Alice but he did not turn around.

Finally, Maule spoke, "Behold your daughter."

Pyncheon turned to find Alice sitting with her long, brown lashes closed over her eyes.

"Alice?" he said, his voice rising. "Alice?"

She never moved. She did not stir when he called or touched her or even when panic overtook him and he shook her very hard.

"Villain!" the old man shrieked. "Give her back! Give her back or hang like your grandfather."

"Oh, now it is my crime?" the carpenter asked. "Were you not the man who sold his daughter for the mere hope of getting a sheet of yellow parchment into your clutches?" With that, he silenced Pyncheon.

The carpenter tried to use Alice's trance as a kind of telescope into the spirit world. Alice

professed to see three figures—an old man with blood on his lips and beard, another man with a rope around his neck, and a middle-aged man dressed as a carpenter.

It seemed clear that the man with bloody lips knew the whereabouts of the parchment. He was kept from telling by the two other men. He attempted to shout the answer to Alice, but the other two grasped at his mouth and fresh blood poured forth.

"It seems," Maule said, "this fortune is part of the old Puritan's curse and he cannot help you. You are stuck with this land and this curse."

Mr. Pyncheon was so shocked by what he had seen and heard that he couldn't speak. He managed only a faint gurgle.

"Ah, sir," Maule said, "do you too have old Maule's blood to drink?"

Finally Pyncheon overcame his shock. "Give me back my daughter and go on your way."

"Your daughter?" Maule said. "It seems she is fairly mine. But I am not a harsh man and will leave her in your keeping." He waved his hands and the beautiful Alice Pyncheon awoke from her strange trance.

But Maule never gave up his power over her. He had only to wave his hand and wherever the proud lady was, her spirit passed from her control and she was forced to do his bidding. He might command her to laugh or cry or dance and she would do so, no matter how inappropriate the circumstance.

On the night of Maule's wedding to a laborer's daughter, he called Alice to come and play servant to his wife. She caught a chill that cold, wet night and soon died.

It was only then that Maule felt any remorse. He had meant to humble Alice, not kill her. But his intent mattered little. She was dead.

# Phoebe's Good-bye

Holgrave finished his tale with a dramatic flourish and looked up, expecting to see a smile on Phoebe's face. Instead, her eyelids drooped and she leaned toward him. While telling his story, he had hypnotized the young woman!

For an instant, he stared in fascination. Then, he shook off any urge to study the hypnotic effect. He gave a sharp gesture of his hand instead. Instantly, Phoebe's eyes snapped open.

"Miss Phoebe," he said, laughing, "I cannot believe you fell asleep during my story!"

"No," she said, "I am sure I did not. I don't remember the story clearly, but I know it was full of trouble and thrills. I am certain your readers will enjoy it."

Evening had begun to fall and the air was sweetly cool after the heat of the day. "I do believe," the young artist said, "that I have never seen so beautiful an evening or been so completely happy."

"I have been happier," Phoebe said. "Certainly more cheerful, but this is a charming evening. I wonder what makes it feel special."

"Do you not know it?" he asked softly. "I think it's a secret that I'm only beginning to see."

She looked at him curiously. "I must go in. Miss Hepzibah is not quick at figures. She will give herself a headache over today's accounts if I don't help her."

"I cannot imagine what she will do with you gone," Holgrave said. "Or what any of us will do." He noticed Phoebe's surprise. "Miss Hepzibah told me you were returning to the country," he explained.

"Only for a few days," she said. "I must make a few arrangements and tell my mother that I have found a home here. It is pleasant to live where one is useful and much desired."

"And you surely are," he said. "More than you know. I cannot imagine what may happen with you gone."

"That is twice you have said that," she said. "I wish you would speak clearly. Do you know of some reason I should not leave?"

"No, nothing," he said. "I just have an odd fancy. Don't worry about it. Let us part while we are still friends."

"Is that what we are?" she asked. "I do wonder sometimes." And then she slipped away into the house.

The day came then for her brief trip to the country. She said good-bye to her cousins with tears in her eyes.

"Ah, Phoebe," Hepzibah said, "you do not smile so much as when you came. The time away will do you good. This house is too gloomy and lonesome."

"Come, Phoebe," Clifford called. "Let me see your face." He caught her face between his hands and stared into it for long minutes. "It is enough. You are beautiful, Phoebe. Come back quickly."

Phoebe gave them each a last kiss and slipped out into the morning light. As she walked down the street toward the train station, she was glad to see Uncle Venner join her.

"We shall miss you next Sabbath afternoon," he said. "Come back soon."

"Very soon," she assured him.

"We could not do without you," he said. "It is as if God has loaned us an angel."

Phoebe laughed at the idea. "I am no angel, Uncle Venner. But I will soon be back." And the two parted as their day called them to different places.

# The Scowl and the Smile

In the next days, a storm moved in. It was as if the weather was trying to reflect the gloom of Phoebe's absence. Poor Hepzibah's scowl grew fiercer than ever. Trade at the small shop fell as neighbors whispered that Hepzibah's face soured the drinks and turned the cakes moldy.

For the first days, Clifford took his seat in the parlor. But with no delight in Phoebe's face, no pleasure in the sunny garden, no gazing upon the street from the upper window, Clifford grew more and more restless.

On the fifth morning, he refused to come downstairs at all. But he did seek some small pleasure by playing Alice Pyncheon's harpsichord.

The beautiful music reminded Hepzibah that Clifford had shown musical talent in his youth. Still, how could he play as if fresh from practice? The harpsichord had not been played in Hepzibah's lifetime. How could it still produce such beautiful songs?

Was the sound from Clifford's hands or the ghost of Alice Pyncheon? Legend held that Alice's ghost played to warn of coming death. Hepzibah shuddered at the thought. Suddenly, the music stopped and the shop bell tinkled.

She might have ignored the bell, except she heard the odd rumbling cough that was always the sign of Judge Pyncheon's presence. She hurried to the shop. The judge smiled as if his face alone could replace the cloud-covered sun.

"Cousin!" he called joyfully. "I could not rest on this stormy day without checking to see if you or dear Clifford had a need."

"We need nothing," she said flatly.

"I believe Clifford needs company," the judge insisted. "And I have come to fill the need."

"He has no need for your company."

"You wound me," he said. "I want only to help."

"Stop it!" she shrieked suddenly. "Will you never stop pretending to care about your victim? He suffers from what you did. Is that not enough?"

"I did only what the law and justice demanded," the old man said. "Have I not worked hard these many years to bring Clifford home again? Have I not succeeded?"

"You!" she said. "You did not bring him home. You put him in prison."

The smile fell away from the judge's face. He looked so very much like the portrait of the Pyncheon ancestor that Hepzibah shuddered.

"It is time to be done with this," he said. "I set him free and I have come to see if he shall retain that freedom."

"What are you talking about?"

"Thirty years ago, when our dear uncle died," the judge said, "his wealth fell far short of what

it should have been. He left everything to me, except this old house that is yours in your lifetime."

"What now?" Hepzibah asked. "Do you want to take even this house from me?"

"Certainly not, dear cousin." The smile had returned to the judge's face. "But before our uncle died, dear Cousin Clifford teased me one day. He said that he knew the secret to a great treasure.

"I thought it was the idle talk of a jealous boy, but now I believe it was not. Clifford knows where Uncle Jaffrey's wealth is hidden and he must tell me. The inheritance was not nearly what it should have been."

"You deceived yourself," Hepzibah said, forcing a laugh. "You're dreaming."

"I do not belong to a dreaming class of men," the judge said. "Clifford knows this secret and he will tell me or I will take it as proof that he has gone quite insane. And I will have him taken to a public asylum for the rest of his life."

"It is you who are diseased in the mind," Hepzibah said. "You are an old man with more wealth than he could ever spend. Can you not be happy with what you have? Clifford has no secret."

"We shall see," the old man said, coughing deep in his chest again. "Meanwhile, make your choice quickly as I have other plans today. Do I see Clifford or do I have him taken away?"

Hepzibah saw that she had no other choice. She led the judge out of the shop and the old man sat heavily in the great ancestral chair beneath the portrait.

He flapped a hand at Hepzibah to fetch her brother while he waited. "Time flies! Bid Clifford come to me."

Never had the house seemed so dark and dismal to Hepzibah. She crept up the stairs, staggering under the weight of what she must do. She paused at the arched window and looked out on the street. How she wished there were someone to rescue her.

She knew that if she threw open the window and screamed for help, any who came would be more likely to help the judge. He was seen as a good judge, a respected judge. No one would help Clifford. And for Clifford to face his evil cousin would be like flinging a cracked vase against a granite column. His sanity could not remain intact.

If only Phoebe were here. Hepzibah knew the practical girl could find some answer the old woman had been unable to see. Then she thought of the young artist. He might be counted on to take their side over the judge, so perhaps he could help.

She pulled open a door, stiff and webbed from lack of use, that connected her part of the house and the gable where Holgrave lived. But his rooms were empty. At this time of day, he worked in his public rooms in town.

With nothing more to keep her from her task, she walked to Clifford's door and knocked. Clifford returned no answer. She knocked again and yet again, and still no sound came from inside.

"Clifford, dear brother?" Hepzibah said. "Shall I come in?" She undid the door and entered the room, but Clifford was not inside. When could Clifford have come out of the room? How could she not have known?

She imagined Clifford hearing her argument with the judge and creeping into the street to escape. But how could her brother survive the crowds? Then she had a thought even more chilling.

What if Clifford had walked to the harbor and stared into the deep, black tide. One misstep, one moment of dizziness could pitch him into the icy darkness.

The horror of her thoughts sent Hepzibah screaming down the stairs. "Clifford is gone!"

She threw open the parlor door. In the darkly shadowed room, she barely made out the judge's figure still seated in the ancestral chair. His face was turned toward the window.

"I tell you, Jaffrey," she cried. "You must help me find Clifford."

But the judge did not seem interested in helping. He did not even turn to look at her. Hepzibah flew into a fury.

"Didn't you hear me?" she bellowed.

And in that instant, a figure stepped into sight from the parlor. A figure with a face so white, it glowed as if lit from within. It was Clifford himself, and he wore an expression of joy as he pointed back toward the shadowy chair with a shaking hand.

Hepzibah grabbed his arm. She tried to tug him from the doorway before the judge could see him.

"Be quiet, Clifford," she whispered.

"Let him be quiet," Clifford said, laughing. "It's what he does best now." He gestured again toward the darkness. "And we can rejoice and dance and be free."

Hepzibah fell as pale as her brother, lifting a trembling hand before her mouth.

"Oh no, what is to become of us," she moaned.

"Let us leave," Clifford said, tugging on her. "We will leave the house to Cousin Jaffrey. It suits him best now."

Hepzibah allowed herself to be pushed along until they were standing in the outer doorway.

"What an absurd figure he looks now," Clifford said with a giggle. "Just when he fancied he had me completely under his thumb."

And with that, he pushed his sister outside. Brother and sister left Judge Pyncheon sitting in the old home of his forefathers all by himself.

# The Flight of the Two Owls

In the gray gloom of the rainy day, the odd, shabby couple drew little attention. The chill east wind had set Hepzibah's teeth chattering as Clifford hustled her down the street. She felt adrift. Her role of protector over Clifford had been turned about and now he guided her.

Over and over, Hepzibah whispered, "Am I awake?"

Finally Clifford led her beneath the arched entrance of a great stone building. Though spacious, the building was partially filled with smoke and steam. A train of cars rumbled as they got ready to go.

Clifford pushed his sister toward the cars and helped her climb aboard. A whistle blew.

The engine puffed with short, quick breaths. The train began to move.

"Clifford, is this a dream?" she asked.

"A dream?" he said with a roaring laugh. "I have never been more awake."

The conductor passed, asking for tickets. Clifford handed him a banknote.

"For the lady and yourself?" the conductor asked. "How far?"

"As far as that will carry us," Clifford said. "It doesn't matter, as we ride for pleasure today."

"You've picked a strange day for that," an old man said. He sat on the other side of the car and peered at Clifford and his sister. "A day like this, pleasure is best found at your own hearth."

"I cannot agree with that," Clifford said, his face glowing. "So fine a thing this train is. It gives us wings. On it, you can live everywhere and nowhere."

"I cannot see it," the old man replied.

"Can you not? And yet it is plain to me. A soul needs air and frequent changes of it. There is a wretched gabled house I know, creaky, rotten, dingy, and dark. I picture a man inside beside a cold hearth. He sits stone-dead with an ugly flow of blood on his shirt. What cheerful breath could one draw there?"

"Well, not there, I suppose," the old man said suspiciously.

At that, Hepzibah leaned close to shush her brother. "They think you are mad," she said. "Be quiet."

"I'll not be quiet," he snapped. "I am suddenly full of words and I will say them."

He leaned toward the old man, who leaned away. "The world is full of wonders and change. This train is a miracle. And mesmerism—have you thought of that? You can turn a man's will with that power. And electricity that connects all the world in a moment!"

"Electricity? Do you mean telegraphs?" the old man said, his scowl lightening slightly. "I do approve of that. A great aid in catching bank robbers and murderers."

"Oh, I would not like it for that," Clifford said. "Seems an unfair advantage, doesn't it? And bankrobbers and murderers are just men like you or me."

"Not like me," the old man snapped.

Just then, the train reached a solitary way station and Clifford said, "Hepzibah, let us alight as birds do. We can perch and choose where we might fly next."

And so the brother led his sister off the train. They stood alone on the platform and looked around at the gloomy place they had chosen to stop.

"I am quite tired now," Clifford said. "I give over to you to choose what we must do."

And so Hepzibah sank to her knees and prayed for God's mercy.

# Governor Pyncheon

While his relatives fled into the storm, Judge Pyncheon sat just as they had left him. He held his watch in his hand and the tick was the only sound in the room. The day grew darker but still the judge sat. He never put away the watch nor blinked his eye.

This was to be a busy day but it passed without him. He had intended to deal with the Clifford business quickly. He had no real worry. He knew he would succeed.

After speaking with Clifford, he planned to attend an auction and buy back a small parcel of land that had once belonged to the Pyncheons. Then he planned to buy a new horse, as his had stumbled earlier in the day. It would not be wise for a man of his importance to ride a stumbling horse.

Later he had an appointment to meet with his doctor. He had felt odd symptoms. Sometimes he felt dizzy. And the disagreeable choking seemed to come more often. Still, he was not truly worried. He and the doctor would have a good laugh over his fears.

His most important meeting had been set for the dinner hour. A group of country gentlemen from around the state planned to meet. They would have a good meal and choose who would next be governor.

Who could make a finer candidate than the judge? Who had a better reputation with the voters? He would be Governor Pyncheon of Massachusetts. He was a candidate the group could back with confidence.

But the judge did not make it to any of his appointments. He spent his day in the chair. His gentlemen friends picked another candidate entirely as the judge sat so still with his watch in hand. Day passed to evening. Evening to night. Night moved to morning.

In the morning's dim light, imagine a great group slipped into the room. A gauzy group of all the Pyncheon ancestors who came to stare up at the great Pyncheon portrait affixed to the wall. Picture the Puritan with his face as stern and disapproving as ever in life. Imagine he tugs at the painting but he can do nothing with his ghostly hands.

Imagine each ghost in turn pushes and pulls on the dusty frame. Picture now a ghost mother holding her ghostly child up so that he might grip the frame. But no one can move it. And during all this parade of Pyncheon ghosts, imagine the old wizard himself standing in the corner and laughing.

Then see? The last Pyncheon ghost. It is a portly ghost in fine clothes, the judge himself, who has no more power to move the painting than any other. But this is only imagination of course. The room is still.

A mouse creeps across the floor to stand boldly at the judge's still feet. A fly buzzes closer and closer to the judge's faintly unpleasant smell. It lands on his forehead and walks boldly down the tall highway of the judge's nose to his cheek. Then finally to his wide-open eye.

Through all of this, the fanciful and the all too real, the judge is completely still.

# Alice's Posies

On the day after the storm, Uncle Venner was the first person on Pyncheon Street. He pushed his wheelbarrow from house to house, picking up the scraps left in crocks and pots. These he fed to his pig.

Someday, when he was too old to work, he promised to throw a grand party where there would be spare ribs and chops for everyone. So everyone on the street contributed to that party by saving scraps for the pig.

When he reached the old Pyncheon house, Uncle Venner wheeled around to the garden and hefted the lid from the crock.

"Well, that's not like Miss Hepzibah!" he exclaimed as he stared into the empty crock.

As he considered knocking, Holgrave leaned out his window and called down, "Good morning, is no one about?"

"Not a soul," Uncle Venner said. "But that wicked storm kept me awake. If Miss Hepzibah had a sleepless night as well, I thought she might have slept in."

"She might," the young man agreed. "I heard such rumbling and banging as the wind rushed around the house. I can't imagine she slept much in that."

"As I thought. Well, I'll come back." He turned his wheelbarrow, then paused. "You know. I saw Alice's posies blooming. If I were a young man such as yourself, I would pick a few and keep them in water until Miss Phoebe returns." Then he winked at Holgrave and slipped through the gate.

After a while, a large woman stomped up to the door of the shop and tried the knob. When she found it locked, she pounded and ranted until she quite wore herself out.

"You'll find no one there, Mrs. Gubbins," called the old lady who lived across the street. "I saw old Hepzibah and Clifford go away yesterday. I expect they've gone to visit their cousin the judge."

"I think not," Mrs. Gubbins snapped. "There's bad blood there, you know. I expect Hepzibah is angry about being so poor while the judge is so rich."

"Perhaps," the neighbor said more timidly. "Still they're gone—that's one thing certain."

Throughout the day, more people sought out the house. Some came hoping to buy, including little Ned Higgins in search of more gingerbread. Some came hoping to deliver items ordered for the shop. All were deeply shocked to find no answer to their knock!

The quiet house was not the only mystery that day. The judge's horse had never been picked up from the stable. People began to talk. Where was the judge?

The last to come seeking something from the old house was the young Italian with the monkey and the music box. He stood grinding away for some time, hoping for a glimpse of Phoebe's face at the upstairs window and a shower of pennies. None came, since the only occupant of the house would not have liked the music even when alive.

Imagine a moment old Judge Pyncheon shambling out to complain about the noise. See the bloody shirtfront and the grim frown on his stark white face. No, it was better for no answer to come from inside.

A pair of local men walked down the street and called to the young Italian, "Be off with you. The owner of the house has been murdered. Everyone is saying it. They'll be no coins for you today. Not from the Pyncheon house."

As the younger man packed up his rig, he spotted a bit of card next to the door of the house. He walked over and picked it up. Then he handed it over to the men.

It was the judge's card, scrawled along the back with a list of the appointments the judge had meant to complete. The old man must have dropped it when he pounded on the door.

"Look here, Dixey," cried the man. "This has something to do with the judge. Here's his name right on it."

"We should take it to the city marshal," Dixey said. "Perhaps the judge went in that door and never came out. His cousin might be up to his old tricks again." He shook his head. "Bad business this. Bad business."

The two men hurried away, scattering a group of children in their wake. The children had heard the men and now stared up at the house, imagining all manner of ghosts.

Just then, a cab drove down the street to stop before the old house. The driver carried a trunk and bags to the house door. A pretty girl in a straw bonnet stepped from the cab. Phoebe was home.

Finding the front door closed and no one answering, she turned to the shop door. It was equally tight against her. As it was a beautiful day, she thought perhaps Hepzibah had decided to devote the day to her brother's joy in the garden.

Phoebe hastened to the garden gate, fully expecting to find the old couple inside. But the garden was quietly neglected and the only ones to greet her were the chickens, who seemed overexcited by her presence.

Phoebe walked to the door that led from house to garden. She knocked and the door was drawn open partway. This was the most frequent way Hepzibah opened doors so that she might let Phoebe in without exposing herself to anyone's view. Phoebe was certain it was her cousin behind the door and the mystery of the day was about to be solved.

With no hesitation, she stepped across the threshold and the door closed behind her.

As Phoebe entered the gloom of the house from the brightness of the yard, she couldn't make out who had welcomed her. Then a hand grasped hers with a firm but gentle pressure and led her into the grand reception room of the seven gables.

The room was empty of all but dust on the floor. Light shone bright through its many uncurtained windows and Phoebe turned to face Holgrave, who held her hand. He looked paler than usual, but he smiled at her with warmth and joy.

"I ought not to rejoice to see you at such a time," he said. "But I do."

"What has happened?" she exclaimed. "Where are Hepzibah and Clifford?"

"Gone. I don't know where."

"That's not possible." Phoebe tried to edge around Holgrave toward the door. "Why are we not in the parlor? I need to look for my cousins."

"You must be strong, Phoebe," Holgrave said, hesitating. It seemed wrong to bring something so horrible into the life of someone so full of brightness. "Something has happened. Not to Hepzibah or Clifford." He pulled out a picture and held it. "I took this in the parlor within the half hour."

"This is death!" Phoebe shuddered, turning very pale. "Judge Pyncheon is dead."

"I believe his death is natural. It seems to be that which has visited the Pyncheons before," the young man said. "But it will look very bad if the body is discovered while Hepzibah and Clifford are missing. People will think only of what Clifford's past suggests."

"But Clifford could do no one harm," Phoebe said. "We know that."

"We do," Holgrave said. "And if they will just return, I believe that the examiners will see that the judge died naturally—and thus their uncle did as well. This could erase the blot on Clifford's past. If only they would come."

"We cannot wait," Phoebe said. "That would be wicked. We must call the authorities."

"You are right, Phoebe," he said. "Doubtless, you are right."

But still he paused. He didn't want to shatter the moment between them. The feel of Phoebe's hand in his. The sense of the two of them, alone holding a secret against the world.

"In all our lives, there can never be another moment like this," he said. "It is not the time, but it must be the time. I must say it. Phoebe, I love you."

She blinked at him in surprise, distracted suddenly from the horror of the moment. "How can that be?" she asked. "A simple girl like me could only make you unhappy."

"You are my only possibility of happiness," he said.

"But you crave a life of constant change," she said. "I could not live that way."

"I wanted change only because I was restless with being alone," he said. "Be with me and I will want only for the world to stop and never move again."

"I would not have you change for me," she said.

"Do you love me?" he asked.

"I do," she said. "You know I do."

"Then I am ready to meet the world and do what must be done," Holgrave said.

At that moment, the front door creaked open though it had been locked fast. Footsteps sounded in the hall, but far too hesitant to be the bold feet of the authorities.

"It is they!" Phoebe shouted and she raced to meet Hepzibah and Clifford where they waited near the door. Hepzibah burst into tears as Phoebe embraced them.

"Our own little Phoebe," Clifford said. "And look, Holgrave with her. I thought of you both when we came down the street and saw Alice's posies in full bloom." He looked from one young face to the next. "And it seems flowers are not all that is blooming in this dark, dreary house."

# The Departure

The sudden death of the honorable Judge Pyncheon created a brief but glorious sensation. It seems that no part of a person's life is so easily forgotten as their death. As soon as the authorities decided that the judge's death was natural, interest in him died away.

An interesting thing did occur. As often happens, the judge's death seemed to give people a truer idea of his character than ever they had in life. And the natural death of the judge, so very similar to the death of the judge's uncle brought talk of a long-ago scandal.

The facts of the case long ago were simple. Old Jaffrey Pyncheon's private apartments were found ransacked and robbed. The old man lay on the floor with blood staining the front of his pale linen.  A bloody handprint proved someone had been in the room at the time of his death.  The likely culprit appeared to be young Clifford since he lived with his uncle.

Now a new theory arose, helped along by Holgrave.  In childhood, Judge Pyncheon had been a favorite of his Uncle Jaffrey, but over time he fell out of favor.  So one night, he snuck into his uncle's home to take what his uncle clearly refused to give.

The old man discovered his nephew searching his rooms and was struck with the family curse by his shock.  It was a natural death.  In a rush, the young man finished his search of the room.  He carried away a will that made Clifford the sole heir to the Pyncheon fortune.  He put in its place an older will with quite a different heir.  Then he snuck out of the house and left the rooms a wreck.

So clearly did the room suggest foul play and so clearly was Clifford a suspect that the real wrongdoer barely needed to lie at all during the proceedings.

Many muttered that the judge had died from the curse for his wrongdoing. Still, it must be said that his death turned into a blessing for several others. By his misfortune, Clifford became rich. So did Hepzibah. So did our dear Phoebe and through her, Holgrave.

Money wasn't the only good result, for Clifford found the departure of his enemy beneficial. He did not become normal, but he was more clearheaded. And he was happy.

Very soon after their change in fortune, Clifford, Hepzibah, and Phoebe decided to move from the dismal old house to the elegant country home of the late judge. On the day set for their departure, they assembled in the parlor with their dear friend Uncle Venner.

"It seems an odd thing to have a cheerful gathering under such a gloomy glare," Holgrave said, gesturing toward the portrait of the scowling Puritan.

"That picture," Clifford said. "Whenever I look at it, I almost remember something about a secret. Perhaps it was a dream from when I was child. I can't remember."

"Perhaps I can help," Holgrave said as he put his finger on the edge of the frame and pushed, releasing a secret spring. At one time, the spring would have made the portrait swing out, but over the years in the damp house the mechanism had rusted. Instead, the portrait fell facedown on the floor.

Behind the portrait they found a dusty sheet of parchment in a small opening in the wall. Holgrave opened the parchment and they could see it was the famous deed to the vast territory eastward.

"This is the parchment that Alice Pyncheon's father wanted more than the safety of his daughter," Holgrave said.

"This is Clifford's secret," Hepzibah said. "But this is worthless except as history. The judge tormented us for nothing."

"I remember now," Clifford said. "I discovered the spring when I was boy. I loved imagining all kinds of treasure in the little hole."

Phoebe looked pointedly at Holgrave. "How did know about the secret spot when even Hepzibah did not know?"

"It is the only inheritance from my ancestors," Holgrave said. "The son of the executed Matthew Maule constructed the recess to hide the documents he stole. He didn't want the Pyncheon wealth. He wanted only to punish them for the death of his father."

"And now the whole claim is not worth one man's share of my farm, the poorhouse where I will soon go," Uncle Venner said.

"Uncle Venner," Phoebe cried, "a lovely little cottage lies in our new garden! We'd like you to come and live there as soon as we furnish it for you."

"You must come," Clifford urged. "I want you always to be within five minutes of a chat with me. Your wisdom will keep me well."

"Dear me," cried Uncle Venner. "You are welcome to any wisdom I might have!"

Just then a plain but handsome carriage drew up before the old mansion. The group hurried outside. Uncle Venner watched as the others piled into the carriage, laughing and chatting. Two men stood at the corner of the street as the carriage pulled away.

"What do you think of that, Dixey?" one said. "My wife kept a shop for five months and lost five dollars. Old Maid Pyncheon kept her shop about as long and now she's rich."

"Pretty good business," Dixey agreed. "Pretty good business."

And at that, Uncle Venner stepped away from the porch of the old house, smiling. He was certain he could hear music. Perhaps the ghost of Alice Pyncheon sat at her harpsichord and played in salute of the happiness that had finally come to the House of the Seven Gables.